THE REAL
MOTHER
GOOSE®

ANNIVERSARY EDITION

Illustrated by
Blanche Fisher Wright

Cartwheel BOOKS®

SCHOLASTIC INC.
New York   Toronto   London   Auckland   Sydney
Mexico City   New Delhi   Hong Kong   Buenos Aires

This book was originally published in 1916.

Published by Scholastic Inc.
SCHOLASTIC, CARTWHEEL BOOKS, THE REAL
MOTHER GOOSE, the CHECKERBOARD DESIGN,
and associated logos are trademarks and/or
registered trademarks of Scholastic Inc.

ISBN 0-439-85875-5

12 11 10 9 8 7 6 5 4 3 2   06 07 08 09 10

Book design by Two Red Shoes Design
Printed in Singapore   46

This Scholastic edition first printing, April 2006

Table of CONTENTS

ANIMALS

Hey, diddle, diddle!
The cat and the fiddle,
The cow jumped over the moon;
The little dog laughed
To see such sport,
And the dish ran away with the spoon.

Hark, hark! The dogs do bark!
The beggars are coming to town:
Some in jags and some in rags
And some in velvet gown.

Bow-wow-wow!
Whose dog art thou?
Little Tom Tinker's dog,
Bow-wow-wow!

Hey, my kitten, my kitten,
And hey, my kitten, my deary!
Such a sweet pet as this
Was neither far nor neary.

"Pussycat, pussycat, where have you been?"
"I've been to London to look at the queen."

"Pussycat, pussycat, what did you there?"
"I frightened a little mouse under the chair."

Sing, sing, what shall I sing?
Cat's run away with the pudding string!
Do, do, what shall I do?
The cat has bitten it quite in two.

Little Bo-Peep has lost her sheep
And can't tell where to find them.
Leave them alone, and they'll come home,
Wagging their tails behind them.

Baa, baa, black sheep,
Have you any wool?
Yes, sir, I have some,
Three bags full:

One for my master,
One for my dame,
But none for the little boy
Who cries in the lane.

A little boy went into a barn
And lay down on some hay.
An owl came out and flew about,
And the little boy ran away!

I had two pigeons, bright and gay;
They flew from me the other day.
What was the reason they did go?
I cannot tell, for I do not know.

Goosey, goosey, gander,
Whither do you wander?
Upstairs and downstairs
And in my lady's chamber.

Hickety, pickety, my black hen,
She lays eggs for gentlemen;
Gentlemen come every day
To see what my black hen does lay.

A duck and a drake,
And a halfpenny cake,
With a penny to pay the old baker.
A hop and a scotch
Is another notch,
Slitherum, slatherum, take her.

Cock-a-doodle-do!
My dame has lost her shoe,
My master's lost his fiddlestick
And knows not what to do.
Cock-a-doodle-do!
What is my dame to do?
Till master finds his fiddlestick,
She'll dance without her shoe.

Mary had a pretty bird,
Feathers bright and yellow,
Slender legs – upon my word,
He was a pretty fellow!

Swan, swan, over the sea;
Swim, swan, swim!
Swan, swan, back again;
Well swum, swan!

Ladybird, ladybird, fly away home!
Your house is on fire, your children all gone,
All but one, and her name is Ann,
And she crept under the pudding pan.

About the bush, Willie,
About the beehive;
About the bush, Willie,
I'll meet thee alive.

A swarm of bees in May
Is worth a load of hay;
A swarm of bees in June
Is worth a silver spoon;
A swarm of bees in July
Is not worth a fly.

Ride a cockhorse to Banbury Cross
To see a fine lady upon a white horse;
Rings on her fingers and bells on her toes,
She shall have music, wherever she goes.

I had a little pony,
His name was Dapple-Gray;
I lent him to a lady
To ride a mile away.

A farmer went trotting
Upon his gray mare,
Bumpety, bumpety, bump!
With his daughter behind him
So rosy and fair,
Lumpety, lumpety, lump!

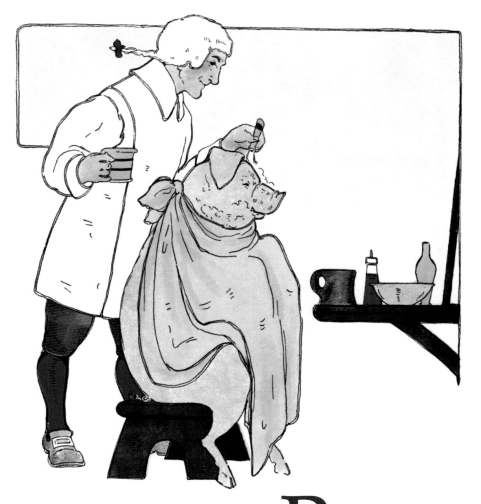

Barber, barber, shave a pig.
How many hairs will make a wig?
Four-and-twenty, that's enough.
Give the barber a pinch of snuff.

To market, to market, to buy a fat pig,
Home again, home again, jiggety jig.
To market, to market, to buy a fat hog,
Home again, home again, jiggety jog.
To market, to market, to buy a plum bun,
Home again, home again, market is done.

Dickory, dickory, dare,
The pig flew up in the air;
The man in brown
Soon brought him down,
Dickory, dickory, dare.

Hickory, dickory, dock!
The mouse ran up the clock;
The clock struck one,
And down he run,
Hickory, dickory, dock!

Three blind mice! Three blind mice!
See how they run! See how they run!
They all ran after the farmer's wife,
Who cut off their tails with a carving knife;
Did you ever see such a sight in your life
As three blind mice?

GIRLS AND BOYS

Mary, Mary, quite contrary,
How does your garden grow?
With silver bells and cockleshells,
And pretty maids all in a row.

Little Tommy Tittlemouse
Lived in a little house;
He caught fishes
In other men's ditches.

Jack and Jill went up the hill
To fetch a pail of water;
Jack fell down and broke his crown,
And Jill came tumbling after.

As Tommy Snooks and Bessy Brooks
Were walking out one Sunday,
Says Tommy Snooks to Bessy Brooks,
"Will you marry me on Monday?"

Little Miss Muffet
Sat on a tuffet,
Eating of curds and whey;
There came a big spider
Who sat down beside her,
And frightened Miss Muffet away.

I had a little moppet,
I put it in my pocket,
And fed it with corn and hay.
There came a proud beggar,
And swore he should have her,
And stole my little moppet away.

I'll tell you a story
About Jack-a-Nory:
And now my story's begun.
I'll tell you another
About his brother:
And now my story is done.

Lucy Locket lost her pocket,
Kitty Fisher found it;
Nothing in it, nothing in it,
But the binding round it.

H
ere's Sulky Sue,
What shall we do?
Turn her face to the wall
Till she comes to.

There was a little girl who had a little curl
Right in the middle of her forehead;
When she was good, she was very, very good,
And when she was bad, she was horrid.

A diller, a dollar, a ten o'clock scholar!
What makes you come so soon?
You used to come at ten o'clock,
But now you come at noon.

There's a neat little clock—
In the classroom it stands—
And it points to the time
With its two little hands.
And may we, like the clock,
Keep a face clean and bright,
With hands ever ready
To do what is right.

Little Bobby Snooks
Was fond of his books,
And loved by his usher and master;
But naughty Jack Spry,
He got a black eye,
And carries his nose in a plaster.

Great A, little a,
Bouncing B!
The cat's in the cupboard,
And can't see me.

1, 2, 3, 4, 5!
I caught a hare alive;
6, 7, 8, 9, 10!
I let her go again.

The fair maid who, the first of May,
Goes to the fields at break of day,
And washes in dew from the hawthorn tree
Will forever handsome be.

Spring is showery, flowery, bowery.
Summer is hoppy, croppy, poppy.
Autumn is wheezy, sneezy, freezy.
Winter is slippy, drippy, nippy.

Rain, rain, go away,
Come again another day;
Little Johnny wants to play.

Seesaw, Margery Daw
Sold her bed
And lay upon straw.

Buttons, a farthing a pair!
Come, who will buy them of me?
They're round and sound and pretty,
And fit for girls of the city.
Come, who will buy them of me?
Buttons, a farthing a pair!

See a pin and pick it up,
All the day you'll have good luck.
See a pin and let it lay,
Bad luck you'll have all the day.

What are little boys made of?
What are little boys made of?
"Snaps and snails and puppy-dogs' tails;
That's what little boys are made of."

What are little girls made of?
What are little girls made of?
"Sugar and spice and everything nice;
That's what little girls are made of."

FOOD

Pat-a-cake, pat-a-cake, baker's man!
Bake me a cake as fast as you can.

Pat it and prick it and mark it with a T,
Put it in the oven for Tommy and me.

When I was a bachelor,
I lived by myself,
And all the bread and cheese I got,
I laid up on the shelf.
The rats and the mice,
They made such a strife,
I was forced to go to London
To find me a wife.
The streets were so bad,
And the lanes were so narrow,
I was forced to bring my wife home
In a wheelbarrow.

Molly, my sister, and I fell out,
And what do you think it was all about?
She loved coffee and I loved tea,
And that was the reason we couldn't agree.

Little Jack Horner sat in the corner,
Eating some Christmas pie;
He put in his thumb,
And pulled out a plum,
And said, "What a good boy am I!"

Pease porridge hot,
Pease porridge cold,
Pease porridge in the pot,
Nine days old.
Some like it hot,
Some like it cold,
Some like it in the pot,
Nine days old.

Little Tom Tucker
Sings for his supper.
What shall he eat?
White bread and butter.

A little old man of Derby,
How do you think he served me?
He took away my bread and cheese,
And that is how he served me.

Hot-cross buns!
Hot-cross buns!
One a penny, two a penny,
Hot-cross buns!
Hot-cross buns!
Hot-cross buns!
If you have no daughters,
Give them to your sons.

Peter, Peter, pumpkin-eater,
Had a wife and couldn't keep her;
He put her in a pumpkin shell,
And there he kept her very well.

Jack Sprat could eat no fat,
His wife could eat no lean;
And so, between them both,
They licked the platter clean.

Curly-locks, Curly-locks, will you be mine?
You shall not wash the dishes nor yet feed the swine,
But sit on a cushion and sew a fine seam,
And feed upon strawberries, sugar, and cream.

Georgy Porgy, pudding and pie,
Kissed the girls and made them cry.
When the boys came out to play,
Georgy Porgy ran away.

Hush, baby, my dolly,
I pray you don't cry,
And I'll give you some bread,
And some milk by-and-by;
Or perhaps you like custard,
Or maybe a tart,
Then to either you're welcome,
With all my heart.

Great A, little a,
This is Pancake Day;
Toss the ball high,
Throw the ball low,
Those that come after
May sing heigh-ho!

The Queen of Hearts,
She made some tarts,
All on a summer's day;
The Knave of Hearts,
He stole the tarts,
And took them clean away.

The King of Hearts
Called for the tarts,
And beat the Knave full sore;
The Knave of Hearts
Brought back the tarts,
And vowed he'd steal no more.

Sing a song of sixpence,
A pocket full of rye;
Four-and-twenty blackbirds
Baked in a pie!

When the pie was opened,
The birds began to sing;
Wasn't that a dainty dish
To set before the king?

Humpty Dumpty sat on a wall,
Humpty Dumpty had a great fall;
All the king's horses and all the king's men
Cannot put Humpty together again.

There was an old man of Tobago,
Who lived on rice, gruel, and sago,
Till much to his bliss,
His physician said this:
"To a leg, sir, of mutton you may go."

There dwelt an old woman at Exeter;
When visitors came, it sore vexed her;
So for fear they should eat,
She locked up all her meat,
This stingy old woman of Exeter.

LADIES AND GENTLEMEN

Oh, dear, what can the matter be?
Oh, dear, what can the matter be?
Oh, dear, what can the matter be?
Johnny's so long at the fair.

He promised he'd buy me a bunch of blue ribbons,
He promised he'd buy me a bunch of blue ribbons,
He promised he'd buy me a bunch of blue ribbons,
To tie up my bonny brown hair.

I won't be my father's Jack,
I won't be my father's Jill;
I will be the fiddler's wife,
And have music when I will.

Bobby Shaftoe's gone to sea,
With silver buckles on his knee;
He'll come back to marry me,
Pretty Bobby Shaftoe!

Robin Hood, Robin Hood,
Telling his beads,
All in the greenwood,
Among the green weeds.

Young Roger came tapping
At Dolly's window,
Thumpaty, thumpaty, thump!
He asked for admittance;
She answered him "No!"
Frumpaty, frumpaty, frump!
"No, no, Roger, no!
As you came, you may go!"
Stumpaty, stumpaty, stump!

Nancy Dawson was so fine
She wouldn't get up to serve the swine;
She lies in bed till eight or nine,
So it's, oh, poor Nancy Dawson.

And do you know Nancy Dawson, honey?
The wife who sells the barley, honey?
She won't get up to feed her swine,
And you know Nancy Dawson, honey?

Old Grimes is dead,
That good old man,
We ne'er shall see him more;
He used to wear a long brown coat
All buttoned down before.

Doctor Foster went to Glo'ster
In a shower of rain;
He stepped in a puddle,
Up to his middle,
And never went there again.

That three wise men of Gotham
Went to sea in a bowl.
If the bowl had been stronger
My song would be longer.

There was an old woman
Lived under a hill;
And if she's not gone,
She lives there still.

There was an old woman, as I've heard tell,
She went to market her eggs for to sell;
She went to market all on a market day,
And she fell asleep on the king's highway.
There came by a peddler whose name was Stout,
He cut her petticoats all round about;
He cut her petticoats up to the knees,
Which made the old woman to shiver and freeze.

There was an old woman tossed in a basket,
Seventeen times as high as the moon;
But where she was going, no mortal could tell,
For under her arm she carried a broom.

"Old woman, old woman, old woman," said I,
"Whither, oh whither, oh whither so high?"
"To sweep the cobwebs from the sky;
And I'll be with you by and by."

Old Mother Goose,
When she wanted to wander,
Would ride through the air
On a very fine gander.

There was an old woman of Leeds,
Who spent all her time in good deeds;
She worked for the poor
Till her fingers were sore,
This pious old woman of Leeds!

There was an old woman of Glo'ster,
Whose parrot two guineas it cost her,
But its tongue never ceasing,
Was vastly displeasing
To the talkative woman of Glo'ster.

BABIES

Here sits the lord mayor,
Here sit his two men,
Here sits the cock,
Here sits the hen,
Here sit the little chickens,
Here they run in.
Chin-chopper, chin-chopper,
Chin-chopper, chin!

This little pig went to market;
This little pig stayed at home;
This little pig had roast beef;
This little pig had none;
This little pig said, "Wee, wee!
I can't find my way home."

Dance to your daddy, my bonny laddie;
Dance to your daddy, my bonny lamb;
You shall get a fishy
On a little dishy;
You shall get a fishy
When the boat comes home.

How many days has my baby to play?
Saturday, Sunday, Monday,
Tuesday, Wednesday, Thursday, Friday,
Saturday, Sunday, Monday.

Hush-a-bye, baby, on the treetop!
When the wind blows the cradle will rock;
When the bough breaks the cradle will fall;
Down will come baby, cradle and all.

Hush-a-bye, baby,
Lie still with your daddy,
Your mommy has gone to the mill
To get some meal to bake a cake,
So pray, my dear baby, lie still.

Sleep, baby, sleep,
Our cottage vale is deep;
The little lamb is on the green,
With woolly fleece so soft and clean—
Sleep, baby, sleep.

BEDTIME

Diddle diddle dumpling, my son John
Went to bed with his breeches on,
One stocking off and one stocking on;
Diddle diddle dumpling, my son John.

"What is the news of the day,
Good neighbor, I pray?"
"They say the balloon
Is gone up to the moon!"

The Man in the Moon
Looked out of the moon,
Looked out of the moon and said,
"'Tis time for all children on the earth
To think about getting to bed!"

When little Fred went to bed,
He always said his prayers;
He kissed mama, and then papa,
And straightway went upstairs.

Jack, be nimble,
Jack, be quick,
Jack, jump over
The candlestick.

To make your candles last for aye,
You wives and maids give ear-O!
To put them out's the only way,
Says honest John Boldero.

L ittle Nanny Etticoat
In a white petticoat
And a red nose;
The longer she stands,
The shorter she grows.

"To bed! To bed!"
Says Sleepyhead;
"Tarry awhile," says Slow;
"Put on the pan,"
Says Greedy Nan,
"We'll sup before we go."

Wee Willie Winkie runs through the town,
Upstairs and downstairs, in his nightgown,
Rapping at the window,
Crying through the lock,
"Are the children in their beds?
For now it's eight o'clock."

Early to bed
And early to rise
Is the way to be healthy
And wealthy and wise.

Alphabetical Listing of FIRST LINES